W9-CKP-717

DISCARDED

# Tiger, Tiger, Growing Up

by JOAN HEWETT
photographs by RICHARD HEWETT

CLARION BOOKS ◆ NEW YORK

HIGHLAND ELEMENTARY
SCHOOL LIBRARY

Clarion Books
a Houghton Mifflin Company imprint
215 Park Avenue South, New York, NY 10003
Text copyright © 1993 by Joan Hewett
Illustrations copyright © 1993 by Richard Hewett
All rights reserved.
For information about permission to reproduce selections from
this book, write to Permissions, Houghton Mifflin Company,
215 Park Avenue South, New York, NY 10003.
Printed in Singapore.
The photographs on pages 4, 5, 6, and 7 are by Darryl Bush,
Marine World Africa USA.

**Library of Congress Cataloging-in-Publication Data**
Hewett, Joan.
Tiger, tiger, growing up / by Joan Hewett ; photographs by
Richard Hewett.
p. cm.
Summary: Describes the special care and training of a tiger
cub at Marine World/Africa USA through her first nine months of life.
ISBN 0-395-61583-6
1. Tigers—California—Vallejo—Biography—Juvenile
literature. 2. Zoo animals—California—Vallejo—Biography—
Juvenile literature. 3. Marine World/Africa USA—Juvenile
literature. [1. Tigers. 2. Zoo animals. 3. Animals—Infancy.
4. Marine World/Africa USA.] I. Hewett, Richard, ill. II. Title.
SF408.6.T53H48 1993
636.8'9—dc20 92-9741
CIP
AC

TWP 10 9 8 7 6 5 4 3 2 1

# ACKNOWLEDGMENTS

Our gratitude to Marine World Africa USA, a wild animal park in Vallejo, California, for letting us go behind the scenes, making this book possible.

In particular, we thank Jim Bonde for giving us the go-ahead and Darryl Bush for patiently working out schedules and readily lending a helping hand. For time and expertise so freely given, we also thank Mary Fleming, Lynn Myers, Dr. Laurie Gage, Piper Kimball, Maureen O'Keefe, Mark Jardarian, Ron Whitfield, and last but hardly least the whole Tiger Island crew: Pat Martin-Vegue, Andy Golfarb, Greg Lee, and Jon Minor.

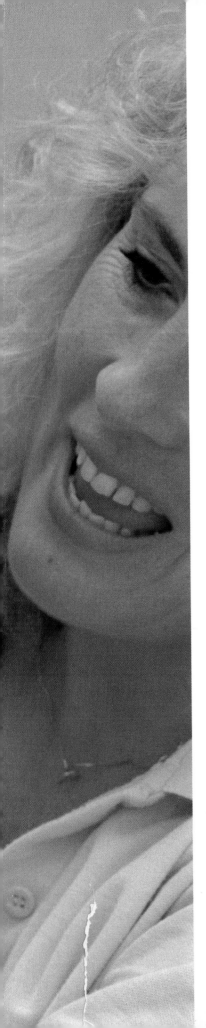

As she wakes up, Tara feels the warm nursery air about her and smells the scent of Mary's hair and skin. Familiar arms cradle her.

Tara knows her bottle is coming. She squeals a loud I'm-starving-and-want-to-be-fed-right-now squeal. Mary smiles at the week-old Bengal tiger cub. "So hungry?" she asks. "Are you so hungry?"

The tiger cub's eyes have not opened yet. She cannot see, but she feels the nipple and begins to suck. The heated, nutritious formula tastes so good the cub is soon sucking with all her might.

"Good girl, good girl," Mary coos.

Before long Tara's little belly is full, and the cub, still sucking, falls asleep. "You're a sweetness," Mary says. Planting a kiss on the cub's head, she lays her back down.

Tara is being raised at Marine World Africa USA, a wild animal park in Vallejo, California. Bengal tigers hunt and roam vast forest lands in their native India. Captive tigers have often been confined to small enclosures where they have nothing to do. In this park the powerful felines are alert and happy, playing and swimming with their trainers. They have been raised to accept people as their friends and protectors.

Tara was born in the park. When she was five days old, she was taken from her mother to be raised in the nursery. Mary and her assistant have fed the cub around the clock.

At nine days, Tara's eyes open. The next day Mary decides it's time for the cub to have a thorough washing. Tigers clean themselves with their rough tongues, like house cats, and tiger mothers wash their young lick by lick.

Mary bathes Tara with warm sudsy water. Despite gentle hands and a quick Turkish-towel rubdown, the outraged cub squalls in protest.

Being a tiger's foster mother seems almost natural to Mary. She has fed, weighed, cuddled, watched, fussed over, and played with sixty other cubs. Tigers usually have litters of two or three. Tara is a single cub and has no brothers or sisters to snuggle with, climb over, and nip, so Mary gives her extra attention.

Each day Mary records Tara's progress. Has the cub gained weight steadily? A look at the record shows that

Tara weighed three pounds when she was five days old
and has made a steady gain of a few ounces daily.

The record indicates when Tara had her first physical
examination and her first series of vaccinations against
disease. Information about Tara's diet is also logged in. From
the medical records of healthy cubs, people in animal parks
and zoos learn how tigers grow and develop.

When Tara is two and a half weeks old, her tiger milk formula is enriched with a small amount of strained baby food. Tara still gets evening and late-night feedings, so before the park closes Mary puts the cub in a carrying case and takes her home.

Though Tara does not like being in her carrying case or in a moving car, the little tiger is happy as soon as she is in the house. Mary is there. Her toys are there. And so is a playpen that is exactly the same as the one in her nursery.

As if she had her own alarm clock, Tara wakes shortly before each scheduled feeding. She plays for a while, drinks her tiger milk formula, and dozes off again. Belly rhythmically rising and falling, Tara breathes heavily and grunts, snorts, and squeals a full array of baby tiger sounds. "You're a noisy one," Mary tells her.

By three weeks, Tara's milk teeth have broken through. Both jaws have several teeth, including incisors (cutting teeth) and pointed teeth called canines (tearing teeth).

Tara soon discovers the joys of chewing. She tries everything: buttons on a sweater, Mary's hair, a ball, an old shoe.

Learning how to behave is part of growing up. In the wild, a mother tiger teaches her cubs the behaviors and skills they need to survive. When their mother leaves the den to hunt for food, the cubs must be quiet so predators do not find and attack them. A cub that cries out is swiftly cuffed by its mother.

In the park, tigers have an affectionate relationship with their trainers, and cubs must learn the behaviors and skills that make this interaction possible. Mary teaches Tara what she can and cannot do.

"No," Mary says each time Tara chomps down too hard. Mary does not raise her voice, but her tone is stern.

"Leave it," Mary says when Tara does not want to let go of a rubber ball or stuffed animal. When Tara drops the toy, they play some more.

Mary encourages the cub to engage in normal tiger behaviors such as pouncing, chewing, climbing, tumbling, and stalking. Sucking on Mary's finger is perfectly acceptable. Mary is an affectionate foster mom. She holds and kisses the cub and encourages her to be affectionate in return. When Tara reaches up and touches Mary's face with a big padded paw, Mary beams with pride.

Eight-week-old Tara is active and curious. If Mary stretches out on the rug, Tara is there climbing all over her. Even though the gangly cub stumbles over her own feet, she likes to explore. When she's put in her playpen, she tries to climb out.

Although Tara doesn't know it, she will soon be ready to go beyond Mary's house and the nursery.

Outside the nursery, the park is filled with visitors. Before Tara is exposed to people and their colds and coughs, the cub goes to the veterinarian for a checkup.

Tara is afraid. There are lights shining in her eyes and the gleaming examining table is slippery. The little tiger roars. It is not her first roar, but it is her loudest. Although the deep vibrating *h-o-w-r* is cute and funny coming from a cub so small, it is a reminder of a full-grown wild tiger's awesome might.

"Well, I'm impressed," the vet's helper says, getting a firmer grip on the cub. The vet listens to Tara's heart; looks at her eyes, ears, throat, and gums; and declares her patient fit.

Tara will soon have two foster mother/trainers. Mary will care for Tara from late afternoon till early morning. Lynn will take care of her during the day. Lynn starts visiting. As she plays with and feeds the cub, her touch and tone of voice are similar to Mary's, and in a few days Tara is giving her loving nips and responding to her commands.

Feeling snug and safe, Tara lets Lynn carry her through the park. Along the way, children excitedly point and say, "Look, a tiger!" Lynn stops to tell them that the tiger is named Tara, and that she is three months old and on her way to her first outdoor enclosure.

Tara looks around uncertainly. The air is filled with interesting smells. She follows her nose and starts to investigate. Romping across the grass and down a slope is fun, but a fallen log looks very strange—and she dashes back to the safety of Lynn's lap.

Playing in the outdoor enclosure becomes part of Tara's routine. Sometimes Lynn collars the cub and takes her for a walk.

After a few turns, Tara gets the hang of walking on a lead. But she would rather roll over and have her belly rubbed, or play a sort of peekaboo game.

Tara adjusts well to new surroundings and new activities. As part of an educational program, park instructors take baby animals into classrooms. Tara will soon be going to school.

There's a buzz in the classroom as Tara is brought in.
Although the students would like to gather around, they
stay seated, listen attentively, and learn that tigers are
endangered.

The instructor explains. Thousands of Bengal tigers were
killed in India in wild game hunts, a once-popular sport.
Thousands more are in danger of dying because their forest
and jungle homelands are being cut down to make room for
farms and houses. India has now turned some forests into
sanctuaries.

If the government can successfully protect these areas, and if the big cats continue to breed, there will still be tigers silently stalking their prey in the dark of night.

All the children say that there should always be wild tigers. And lions. And elephants. And bears.

Now the instructor lets one of the children pet Tara. Several boys and girls want to know how her coat feels. "Is she soft, like a kitten?"

The boy says, "No, kind of rough, like my dog."

Because the instructor handles the cub in a familiar firm but gentle manner, Tara gives the young woman her trust. Still, the visit was exhausting. Tara sleeps so soundly when she gets home that Mary has to wake her for her evening bottle.

Mary has been trying to get Tara to eat meat. She lets the cub have some of her formula first and offers a piece of meat afterward. She withholds the bottle and gives the meat instead. For almost three weeks, the cub remains unconvinced that meat is edible. Then one day she takes a piece on her own.

Tigers can change their habits. In the wild they spend much of the night hunting and sleep in the day. In the park, tigers are active during daylight hours and sleep at night.

Three-month-old Tara sleeps through the night in the nursery and plays outdoors with Lynn during the day.

Tara greets Lynn with an affectionate puffing sound. Sometimes Lynn blows air through her own lips and makes a similar noise, and the cub blissfully puffs back. Through friendly play, Lynn continues to teach the cub what she can and cannot do and to make sure that Tara obeys.

At nine months Tara gets a new set of trainers. They are the men who care for the park's adult tigers.

Tara will not reach her full size until she is two or three years old. Adult male tigers weigh about 475 pounds and adult females about 300. Tara weighs 90 pounds. Still, the adolescent tiger is big enough and strong enough to join the mature felines on their Tiger Island home. The "island" is a moated compound designed for tigers. It has a lawn for running and stalking, shade trees for napping, logs for climbing, and a good swimming pond.

Tigers are solitary animals. In the wild each adult has its own territory. Even in the park they do not develop bonds with one another. But, like Tara, all the park's tigers have been raised by people, and the tiger-trainer bond is reinforced daily.

In less than a year, Tara has outgrown the nursery and her first outdoor enclosure, and has grown into her adult life on Tiger Island.

HIGHLAND ELEMENTARY
SCHOOL LIBRARY